Silly Jack
and the
Beanstack

Anholt, Laurence.
      {Daft Jack and the bean stack}
      Silly Jack and the beanstack / written by Laurence Anholt;
illustrated by Authur Robins.
            p.   cm.
      Summary: In this version of the traditional tale, Jack climbs a
stack of baked bean cans and encounters a giant, an event that
makes his and his mother's fortune in an unexpected way.
            ISBN 0-88166-348-4 (Meadowbrook)
            ISBN 0-689-83070-X (Simon & Schuster)
      [1. Fairy tales. 2. Folklore—England.] I. Robins, Arthur, ill. II.
Jack and the bean stalk. English. III. Title.
PZ7.A58635Si 1999
398.2—dc21
[E]   99-33357
                                      CIP

Text © 1999 Laurence Anholt. Illustrations © 1999 Arthur Robins

Published in Great Britain by Orchard Books under the title
Daft Jack and the Bean Stack.

Published by Meadowbrook Press, 5451 Smetana Drive,
Minnetonka, Minnesota 55343

ww.w.meadowbrookpress.com

BOOK TRADE DISTRIBUTION by Simon & Schuster, a division of
Simon and Schuster, Inc., 1230 Avenue of the Americas, New York,
NY 10020

03 02 01 00 99   12 11 10 9 8 7 6 5 4 3 2 1

Printed in the United States of America

Silly Jack
and the
Beanstack

Written by Laurence Anholt
Illustrated by Arthur Robins

These stories have not been tested on animals.

Meadowbrook Press

Distributed by Simon & Schuster
New York

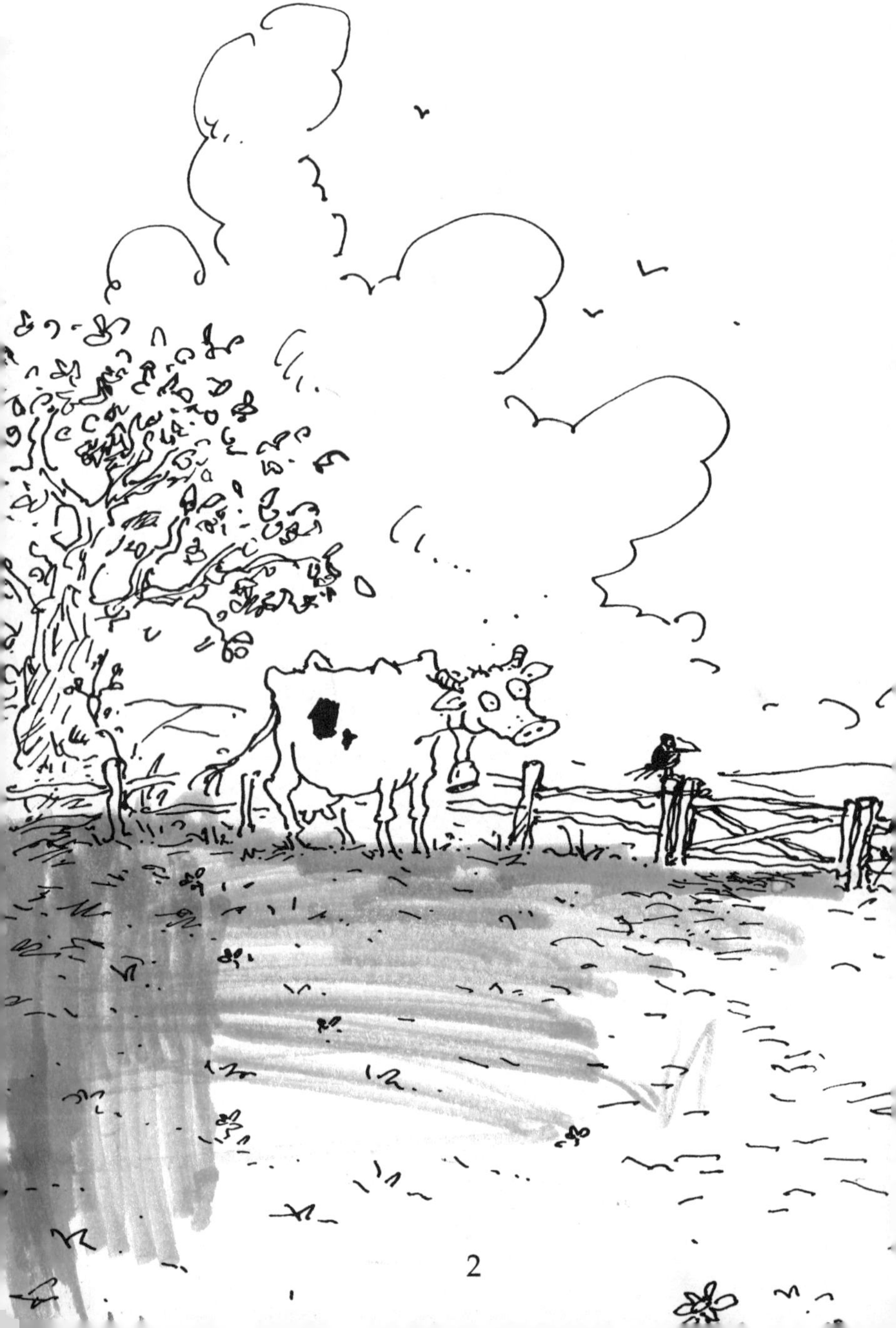

Silly Jack and his mother were so poor . . .

. . . they lived under a cow in a field. His
mom slept at the front end . . .

. . . and Jack slept at the udder end.

Daisy was a good cow, but the problem was, Jack's mom was fed up with milk. It was all they ever had—
hot milk,
cold milk,
warm milk,
milk on toast,
milk pudding.

And on Sundays, for a special treat, they had Milk Surprise (which was really just milk with milk on top).

Jack didn't mind milk, but his mother would have given anything for a change.

"I'M SICK AND TIRED OF MILK!" she would shout. "If I never taste another drop as long as I live it will be too soon. If only you were a clever boy, Jack, you would think of something."

"I have thought of something," said Jack.
"It's a new kind of milkshake—it's milk
flavored."

Jack's mom chased him all around the
field.

One day, a terrible thing happened. Jack was sitting in the field eating frozen milk on a stick and his mom was having her after-milk rest when Daisy suddenly looked up at the gray sky, decided it was going to rain and, as all cows do, lay down.

10

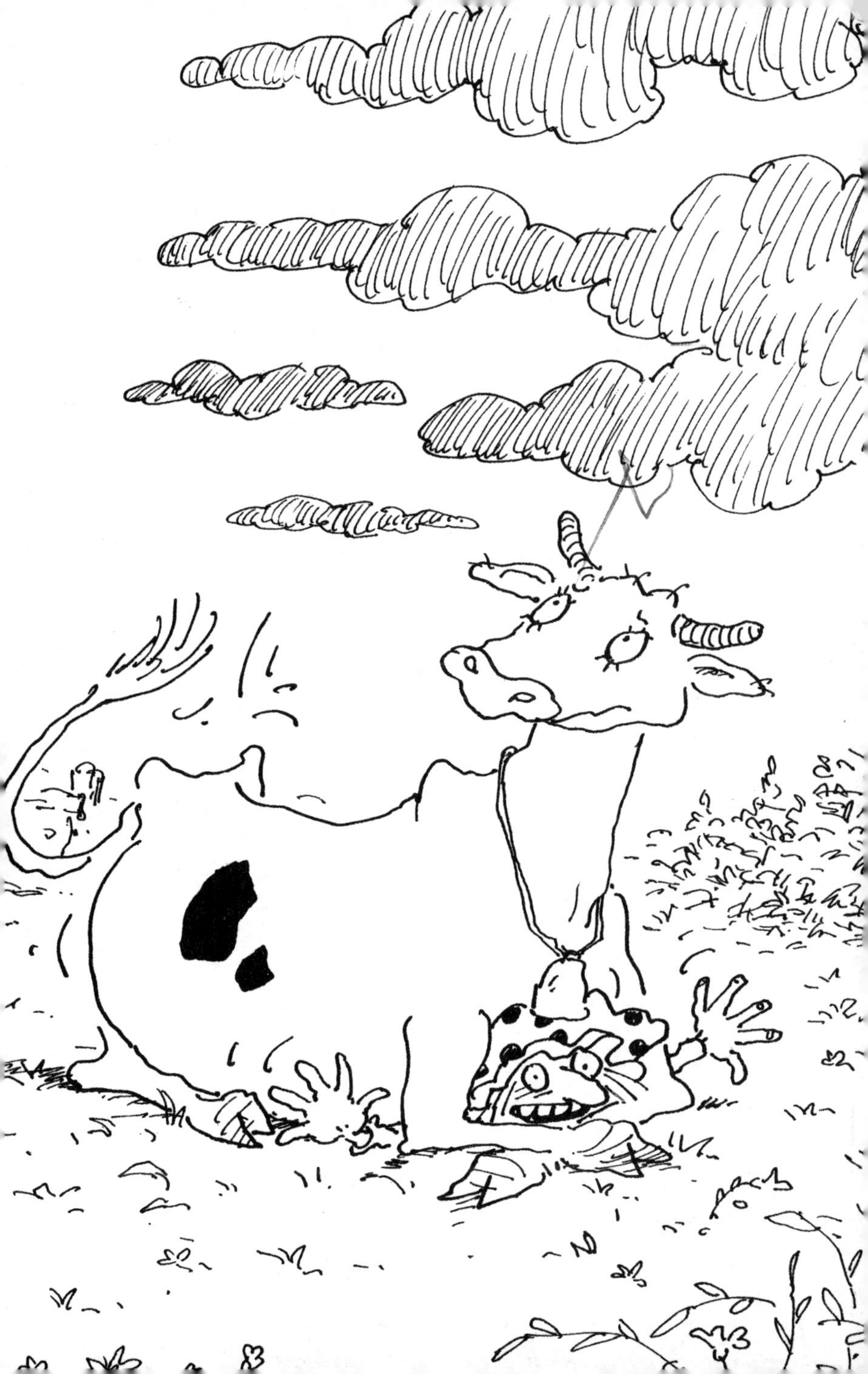

"All right! That's it. I've had enough!" spluttered Jack's mom when Jack had pulled her out by the ankles. "You will have to take Daisy into town and sell her. But make sure you get a good price or I'll chase you around the field for a week."

Silly Jack was very sad because Daisy was more like a friend than just a roof over his head. But he always liked to please his mother.

He made himself a milk sandwich for the journey, then Jack and Daisy set off toward town. It was a long way so they took turns carrying each other.

Then at the top of a hill, they met an old
man sitting on a tree stump with a
shopping bag.

"That's a fine cow you're carrying," he said. "What's your name, sonny?"

"It's Jack," said Jack. "but everyone calls me 'Silly.' I don't know why."

"Well, Jack," said the old man. "I'd like to buy that cow from you."

"I would like to sell this cow, too," said Jack. "But you'll have to give me a good price for her. Otherwise my mom will chase me around the field for a week."

"I can see you're a clever boy," said the old man, "and I'm in a good mood today. So guess what I'm going to give you for that cow?"

"What?" said Jack.

The old man reached into his shopping bag.

"Beans!" said the old man. "Not just one bean! Not just two beans! I'm going to give you A WHOLE CAN OF BAKED BEANS!"

Jack couldn't believe his luck. Not one bean, not two beans, but a WHOLE CAN of baked beans for just one old cow. It was Jack's lucky day! At last his mom would be proud of him.

So Jack kissed Daisy good-bye and set off
home carrying the can of beans as carefully
as he would carry a newborn baby, feeling
very pleased with himself.

As soon as he saw the field he began to shout, "Look Mom! All our troubles are over. Guess what I got for Daisy? Not one bean. Not two beans. But A WHOLE CAN COMPLETELY FULL OF BEANS! Why Mother, there must be A HUNDRED yummy beans in this can. I knew you'd be pleased!"

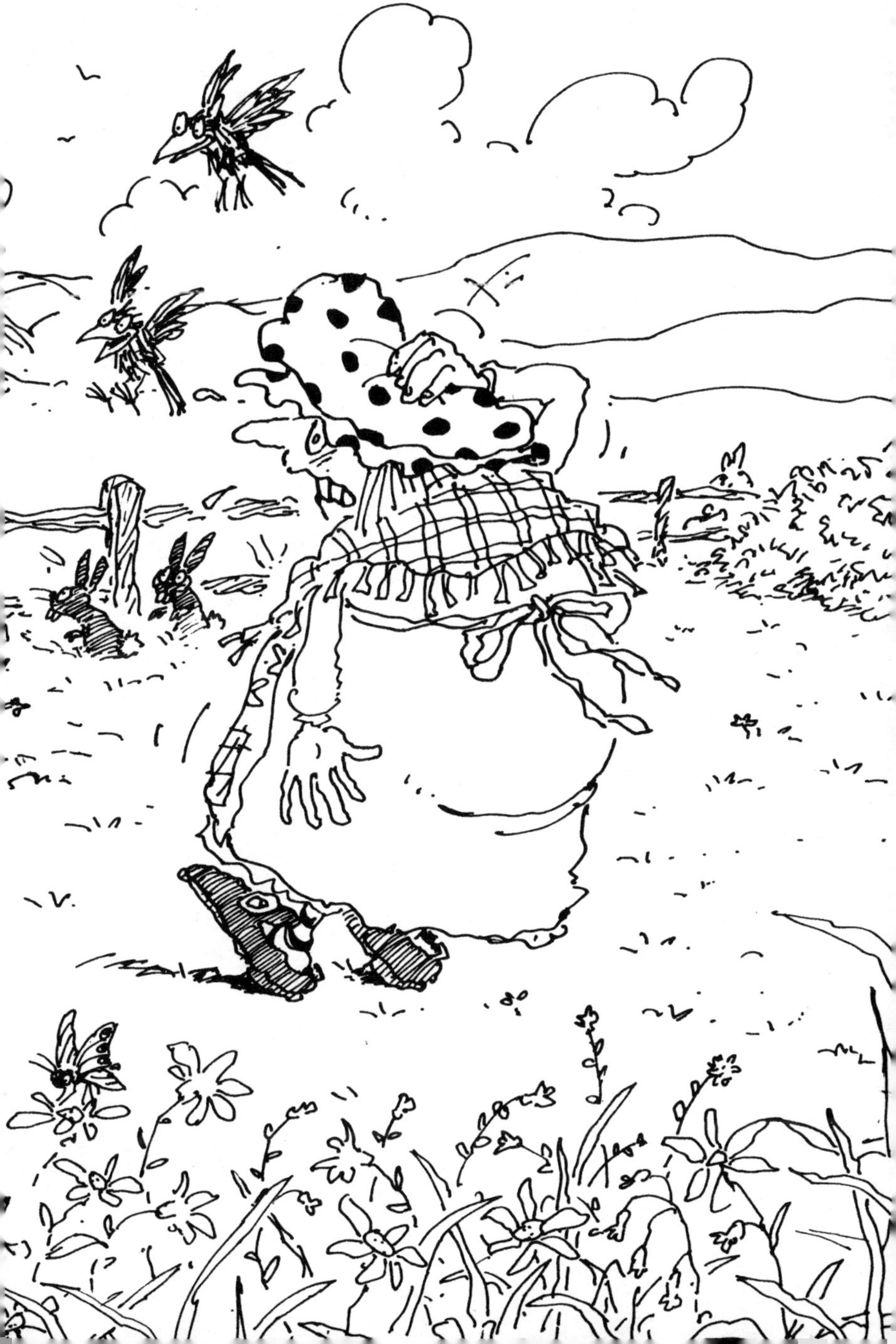

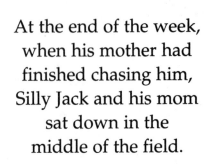

At the end of the week, when his mother had finished chasing him, Silly Jack and his mom sat down in the middle of the field.

"Oh Jack," wailed his mom. "Now we don't even have a cow to sleep under. If only you were a clever boy, you'd think of something."

"I have thought of something, Mom," said Jack. "Let's eat the beans."

So Silly Jack and his mom ate the beans. Then they had nothing left at all.

That night, Jack couldn't sleep. "I can't do anything right," he thought sadly. "My poor mother would be better off without me. I think I will run away into the big wide world and seek my fortune."

So Jack decided to leave a note for his mother. He couldn't find any paper so he tore the label from the bean can. But there was something already written on the back of the baked bean label.

Jack held the paper up to the moonlight and read aloud. . .

Jack woke his mother. When she saw the message on the bean can, she couldn't believe her eyes. "Oh Jack," she cried. "Perhaps we will be able to buy a real house."

"Yes," said Jack, "and perhaps we will be able to buy poor Daisy back. Then we'll have lots of milk."

Jack's mom was too happy to chase him around the field.

In the morning they sent off the lucky bean label and soon their prize arrived—A WHOLE TRUCK LOAD OF BAKED BEANS.

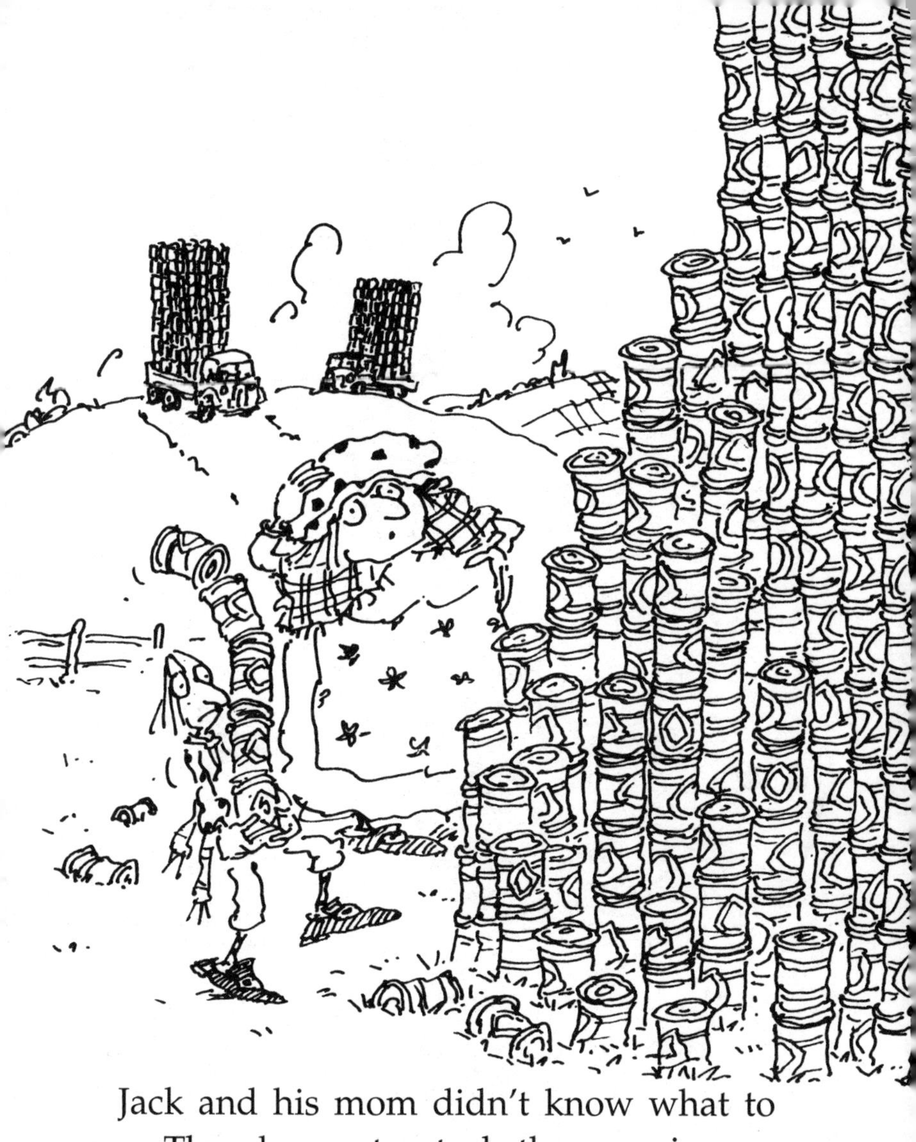

Jack and his mom didn't know what to say. They began to stack the cans in one corner of the field, but before they had finished a second truck load of beans arrived.

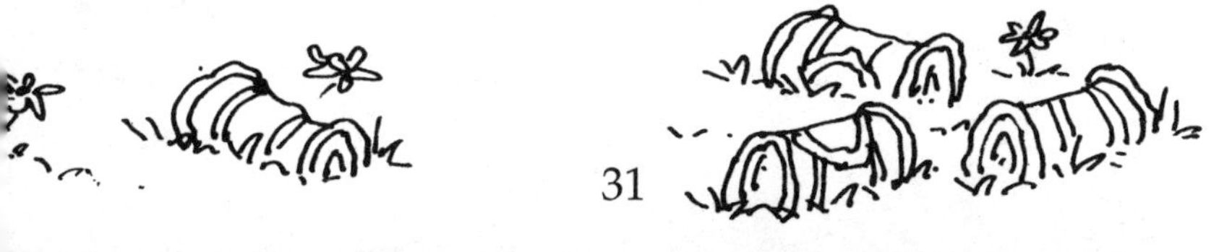

All day long the trucks kept coming. By the evening there was a huge pile of bean cans. A STACK of bean cans. A COLOSSAL GLEAMING MONUMENTAL MOUNTAIN of bean cans. There were bean cans right up to the clouds.

So from that day on Silly Jack and his mom ate beans. It was all they ever had—
hot beans,
cold beans,
warm beans,
beans on toast,
bean pudding.

BEANS, BEANS, BEANSY BEANS!

And on Sundays, for a special treat, they had Bean Surprise (which was really just beans with beans on top).

Jack's mom would have given anything for a change.

"I'm SICK AND TIRED OF BEANS!" she shouted one day. "If I never eat another bean as long as I live it will be too soon. If only you were a clever boy, Jack, you would think of something."

"I have thought of something," said Jack.
"Bean juice milkshake."

There wasn't room to chase Jack around the field because the beanstack was too big. So Jack's mom chased him up the beanstack instead.

Jack hopped higher and higher, from can to can, with his mom puffing and panting behind him.

Soon Jack climbed so high he left his mom far behind. But Jack didn't stop. He kept on climbing. He looked down at the world below. He saw the field as small as a handkerchief and his mom as tiny as an ant. And still Jack climbed higher.

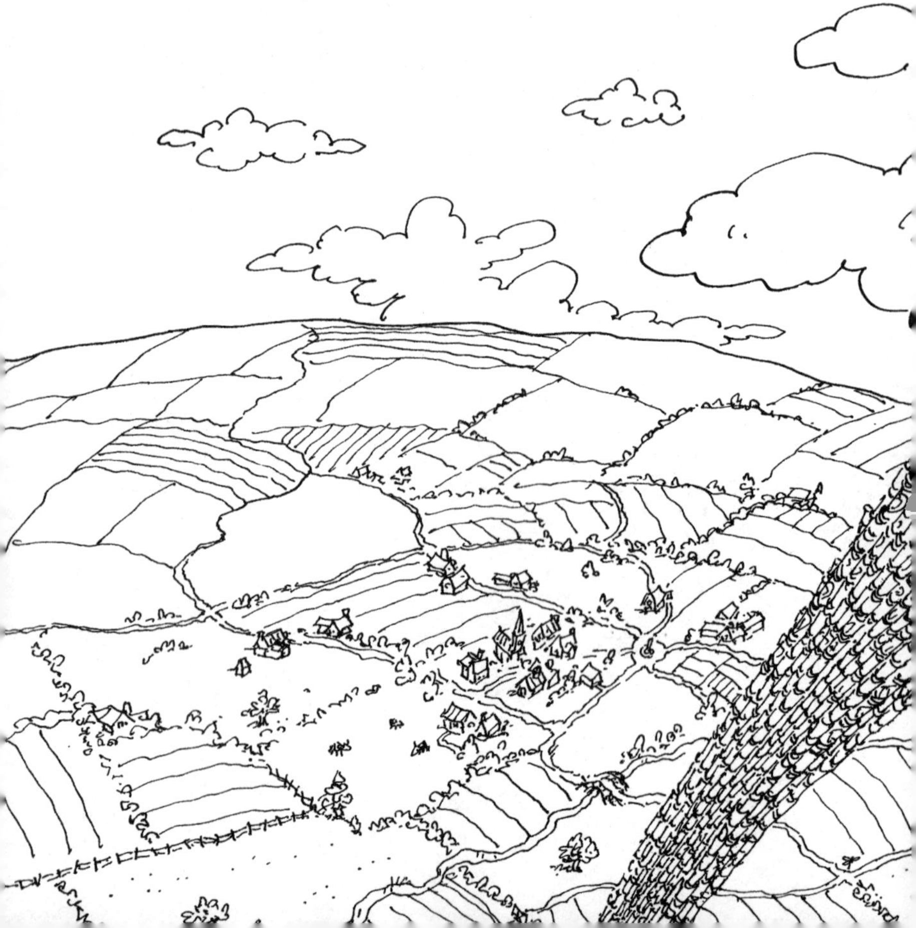

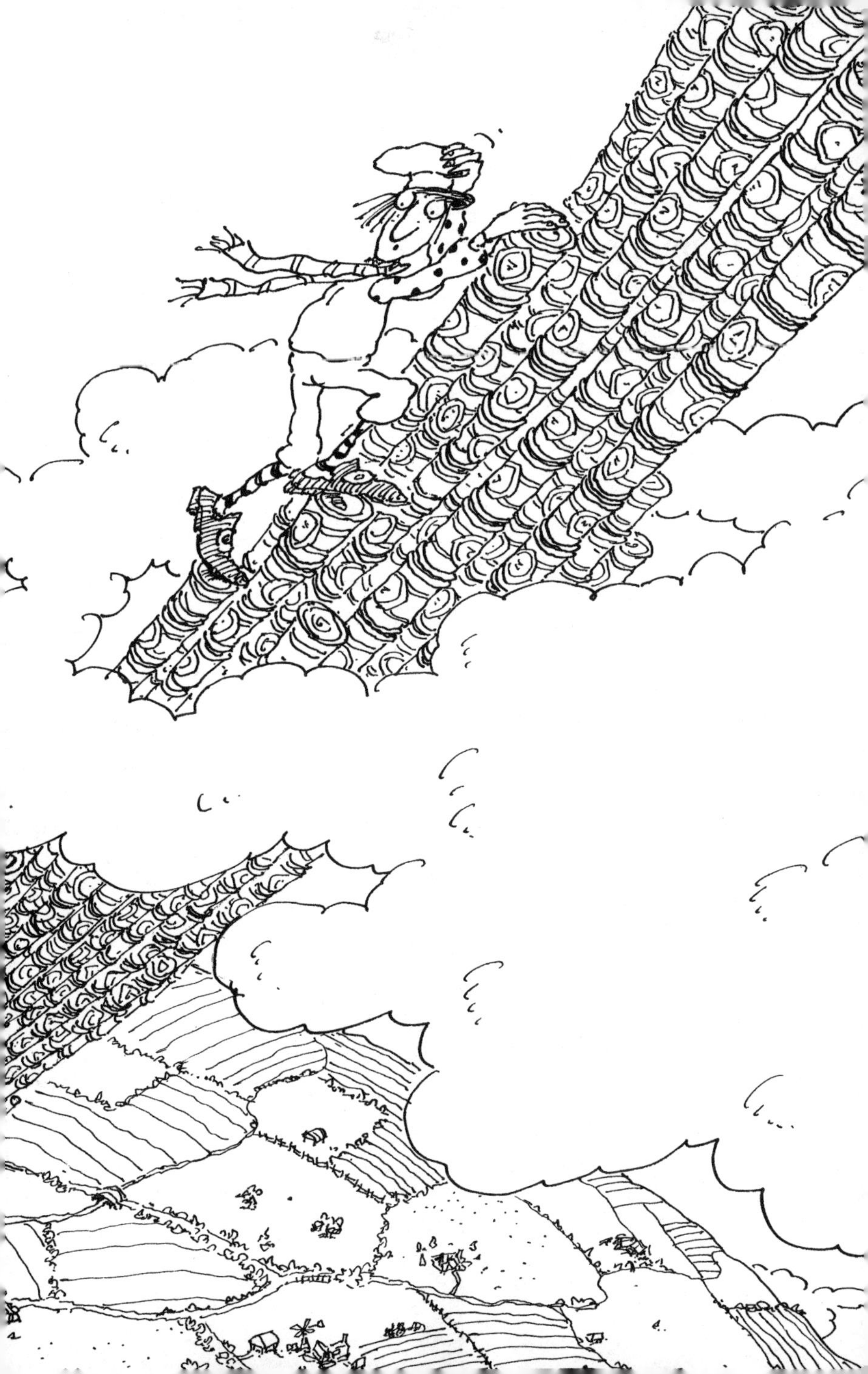

When he was almost too tired to climb anymore, Jack reached the top of the beanstack, way up in the clouds.

Jack looked around. To his amazement
he saw an enormous castle with its great
door wide open.

He tiptoed inside. It was the most
incredible place he had ever seen.

Jack wandered from room to room. He found massive bedrooms with carpets as thick as snow drifts, a solar heated Jacuzzi, a living room with great armchairs, and a TV screen the size of a cinema.

At last, Jack
wandered into a
wonderful kitchen
fitted with every
kind of gadget.

Jack was interested in cooking and he climbed up to look at the giant-sized microwave.

Suddenly, the whole castle began to shake. A great voice roared.

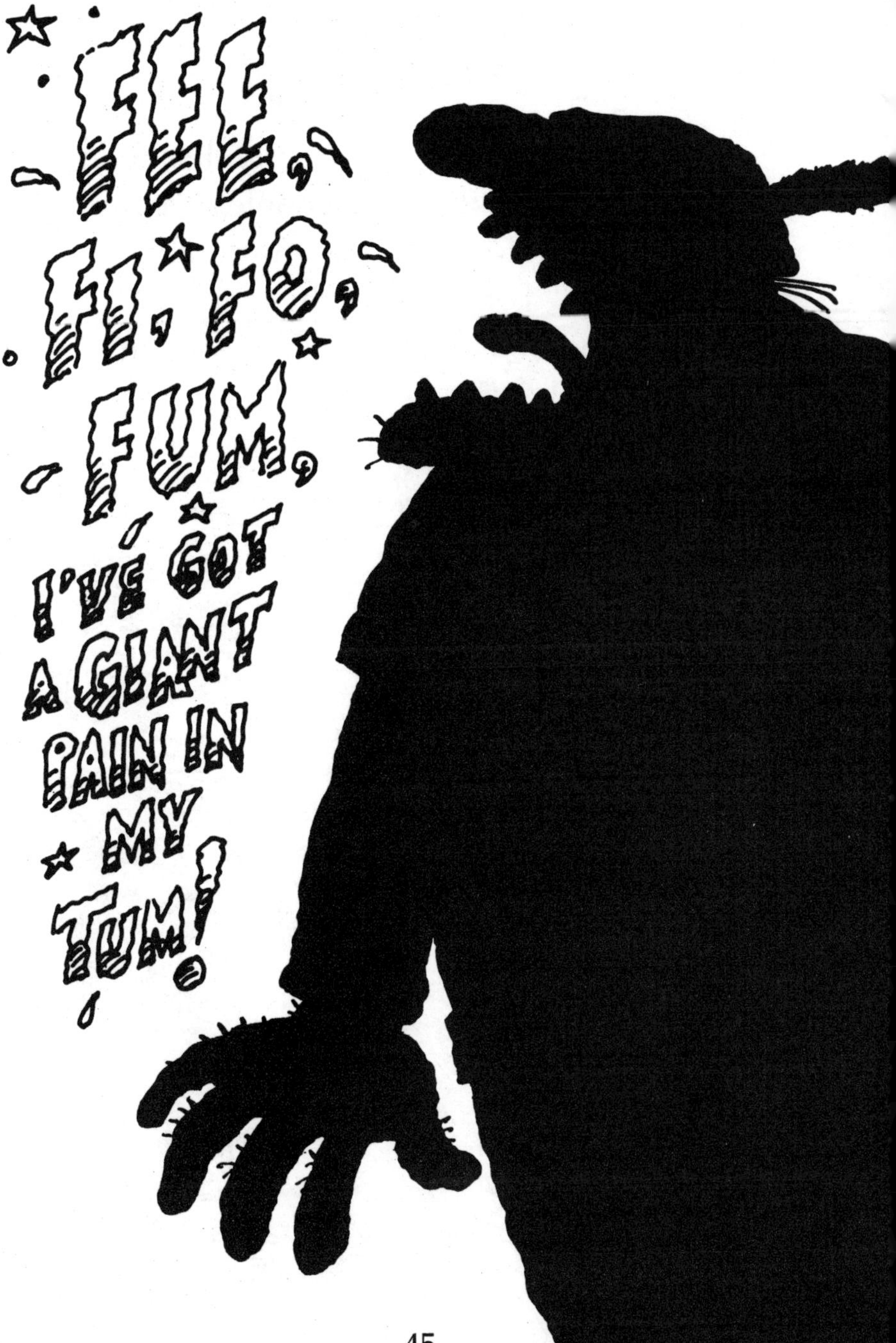
FEE, FI, FO, FUM, I'VE GOT A GIANT PAIN IN MY TUM!

Jack looked around in alarm and saw an enormous giant sitting at a table, rubbing his stomach and looking very miserable.

"S'not fair!" complained the giant. "All I ever get to eat is CHILDREN! And now I've got a belly ache . . .

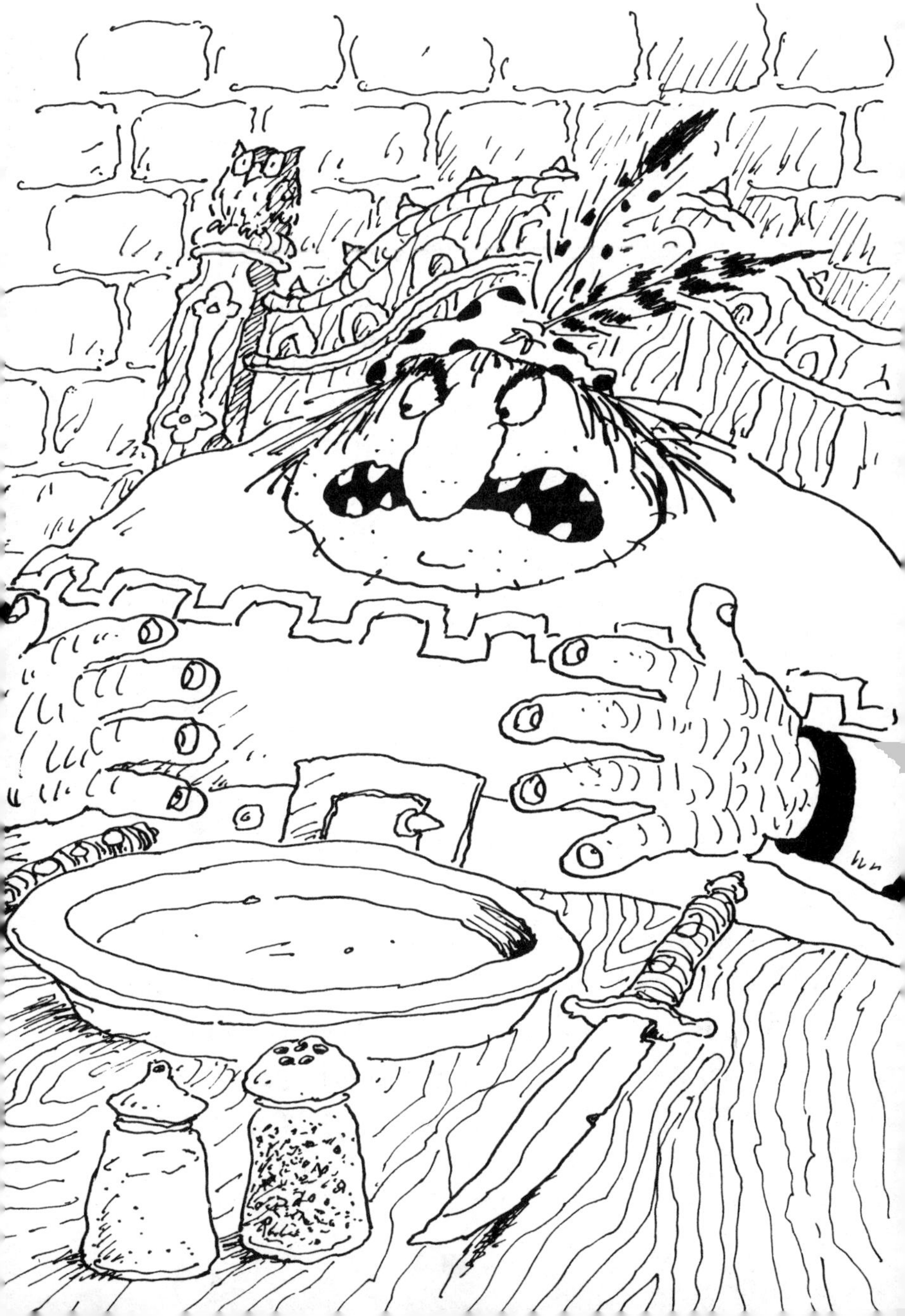

"Hot kids,
cold kids,
warm kids,
kids on toast,
kid pudding.
And on Sundays,
for a special treat,
I have Kid Surprise
(but that's just kids
with kids on top).
I'd give ANYTHING for a change. I'M SICK
AND TIRED OF KIDS! If I never ate another
kid as long as I live it would be too soon . . ."
He looked down at Jack. "AND NOW I'VE
GOT TO EAT YOU TOO! S'NOT FAIR!"

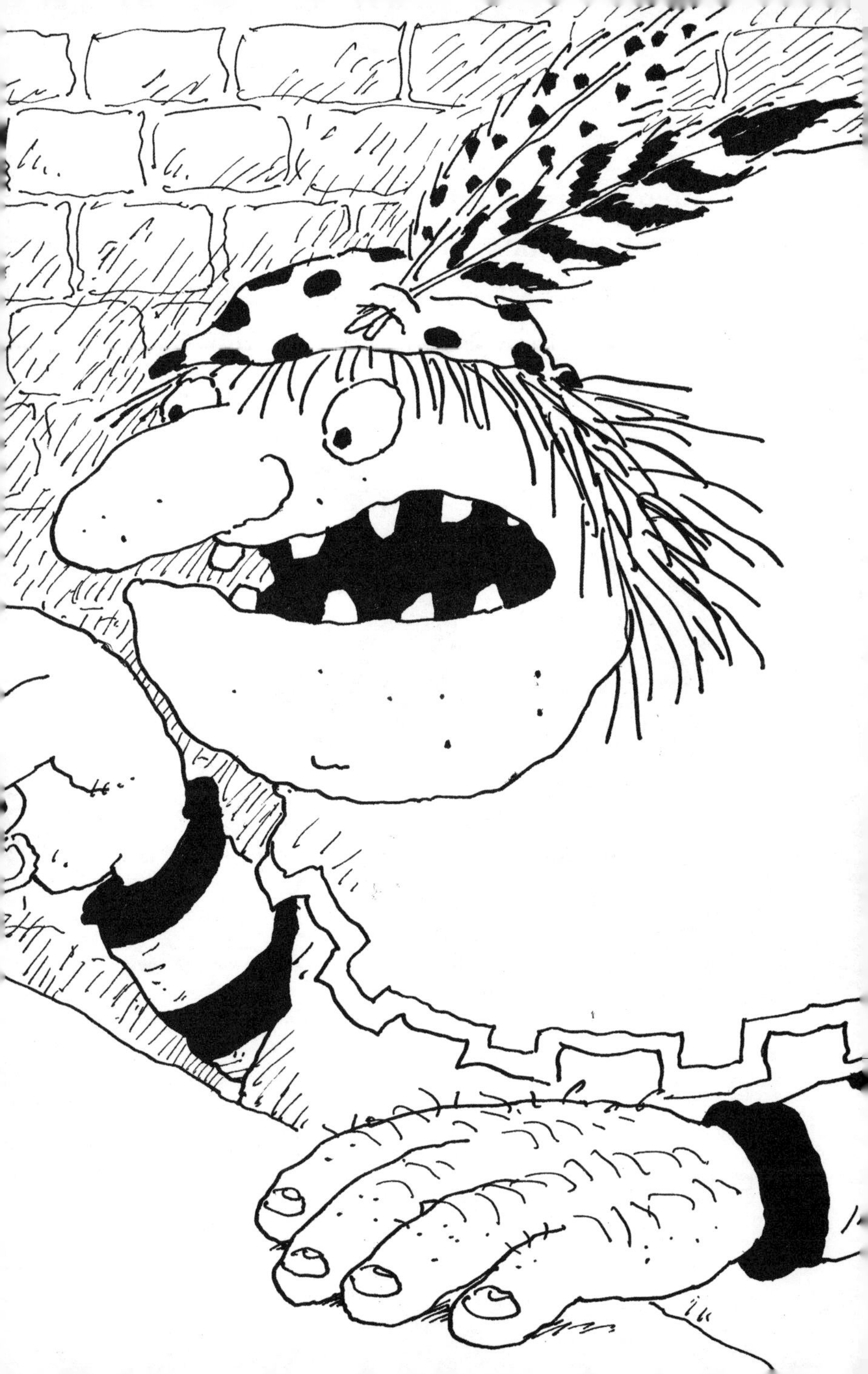

The giant reached out a huge hairy hand
and grabbed Jack around the waist.
He lifted Jack kicking and struggling
into the air and opened his vast black
cave-like mouth with a tongue like
a huge purple carpet.

"Well," thought Jack, "this is the end of
Silly Jack unless I can think of something."

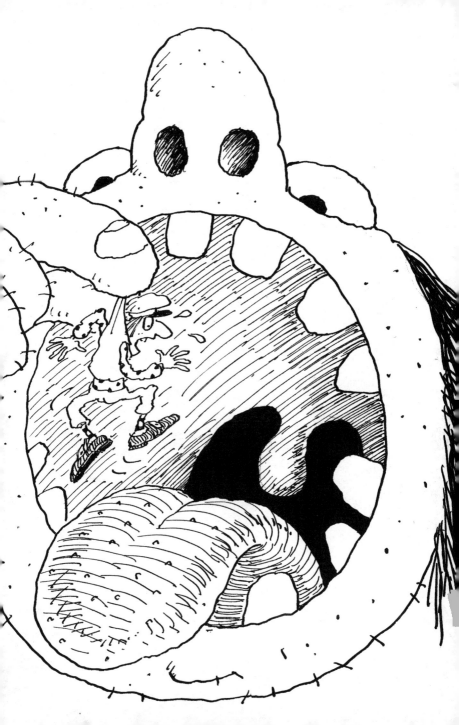

He was just about to be crunched into a million tiny silly pieces, when suddenly he had an idea.

'Er, Excuse me, Mr. Giant,' he whispered nervously. 'If you eat me it will only make your tummy ache worse. I can think of something much nicer. I don't suppose you like...beans do you?'

'BEANS!' roared the giant "DO I LIKE BEANS? I YUMMY YUMMY LOVE 'em!"

So Jack took the giant by the hand and
led him down the beanstack. On the way,
the giant told Jack how lonely he was, all by
himself in the great big castle in the clouds
with nothing to do but eat people.

Jack began to feel very sorry for the poor giant and took him home to meet his mom.

"Oh Jack," she cried. "Where have you bean?"

Jack's mom was very pleased to see Jack in one piece. But when she saw the giant . . .!

And when the giant saw Jack's mom . . .!

It was love at first sight.

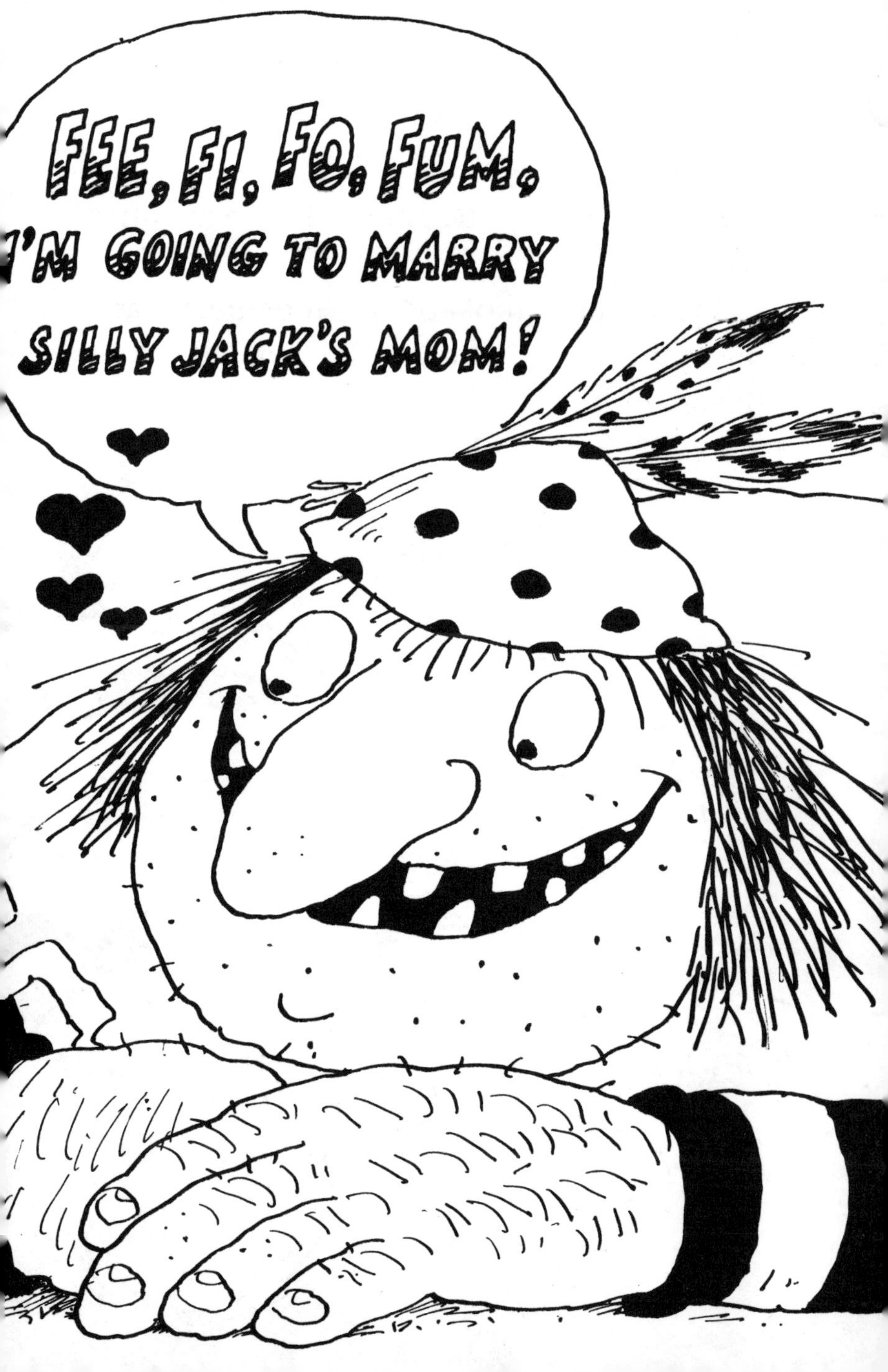
FEE, FI, FO, FUM, I'M GOING TO MARRY SILLY JACK'S MOM!

"Of course you are, dear," said Jack's mom, "but first you must be hungry after your long journey."

The giant looked at the beanstack gleaming in the evening light as he licked his giant lips.

He began munching the beans. Not one can, not two cans, but the whole stack of beans. He didn't even stop to open the cans.

So Silly Jack's mom married the giant, and they were very happy. They all went to live in the giant's wonderful castle in the sky.

Silly Jack opened a cafe in the giant's kitchen and called it "SILLY JACK'S SKY SNACKS." People came from far and wide and Jack grew rich and happy.

He served everything you can think of except milk . . .

and beans.